The Ultimate Guide to Grandmas & Grandpas!

by Sally Lloyd-Jones

illustrated by Michael Emberley

HarperCollins*Publishers*

The Ultimate Guide to Grandmas and
Grandpas! Text copyright © 2008 by Sally
Lloyd-Jones Illustrations copyright © 2008 by
Michael Emberley Manufactured in China.
For information address HarperCollins
Children's Books, a division of HarperCollins Publishers,
1350 Avenue of the Americas, New York, NY 10019.
www.harpercollinschildrens.com Library of Congress
Cataloging-in-Publication Data Lloyd-Jones, Sally, 1960- The
ultimate guide to grandmas and grandpas! / by Sally Lloyd-Jones ;
illustrated by Michael Emberley. — 1st ed. p. cm. Summary:
Provides insights into making your grandparents happy, from singing
and dancing for them to letting them give you special treats and presents.
ISBN 978-0-06-075687-1 (trade bdg.) ISBN 978-0-06-075688-8 (lib. bdg.)
[1. Grandparent and child—Fiction. 2. Family life—Fiction.] I. Emberley, Michael,
ill. II. Title. PZ7.J258Ult 2008 2007020880 [E]—dc22 CIP AC Typography
by Allison Limbacher 1 2 3 4 5 6 7 8 9 10 ❖ First Edition

For Harry and his granny with love
—S.L-J.

To Adrian, for training her grandma
and grandpa so well
—M.E.

When you have a grandma

or a grandpa,

you need to **sing** to them

and **dance** for them

and **paint** lovely
pictures for them.

You need to **scream** and run away when they pretend to be a monster. And let them chase you around the backyard.

hee hee

rroar!

When you have a grandma or a grandpa,

you need to hold their hand when they cross the street.

And help them park the car.

When it's nice outside, it's good to take your grandma and grandpa on picnics

and show them your running ...

and your swimming.

(But you must be able to see them
all the time in case they run off.)

You need to teach your grandma football,
let her score touchdowns, and then shout,

"Good job,
Grandma!"

It's important to let your grandpa have some of your ice cream, and let him build you big sand castles like when he was a boy. (You have to let him sit in them.)

And then you need to knock them over so he can do it again.

You need to make sure your grandma and grandpa have their naps when they're tired.

ZZZZZZZ

zz

ZZZZZZZZZZZZ

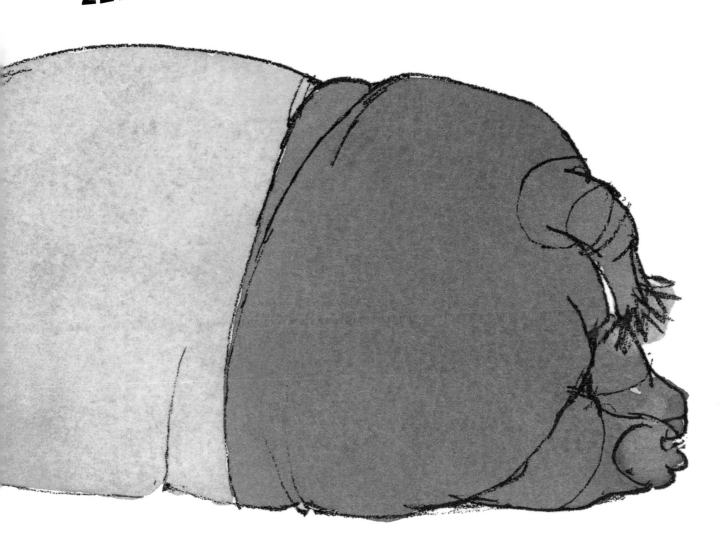

(Sometimes you have to take a nap with them
so they're not the only ones.)

And if they're sick, you must let them borrow
your special blanket.

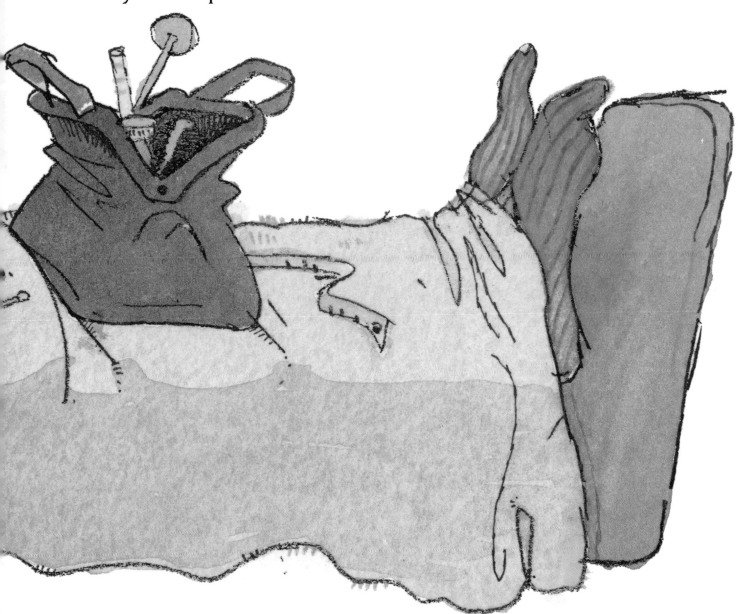

When you have a grandma or a grandpa,
you need to always play with them.

And sometimes let them win.

You need to always love their dinners and eat them up and always ask for more. And let them give you special treats you're not allowed at home.

You must always let them give you presents.
And keep you up too late.

You must sit in your grandpa's lap so he can practice his reading on you.

And before you go to sleep, you need to listen to your grandma's stories about Black Beard and Pirates and *Danger* on the High Seas.

When you have a grandma or a grandpa,
you need to let them make you things.
And tell you secrets about how
naughty your mommy was
when she was little.

And when they throw you up in the sky, a good thing to shout is,  "Again!"

(And then you let them tickle you.)

And, when you wave good-bye, a
good thing to say is, "Au revoir!"
(Which means you'll come back soon.)

But mostly, when you have
a grandma or a grandpa,

you need to **kiss** them.

And **hug** them.

And always
love them.

Because that's what grandmas and
grandpas like best in all the world.